D1405778

For Mimi, with love

M. C. B.

To Lily Grace Connor

T. M.

tiger tales

5 River Road, Suite 128, Wilton, CT 06897

Published in the United States 2021

Text copyright © 2021 M. Christina Butler

Illustrations copyright © 2021 Tina Macnaughton

ISBN-13: 978-1-68010-259-8

ISBN-10: 1-68010-259-1

Printed in China

LTP/1800/3748/0421

All rights reserved

10 9 8 7 6 5 4 3 2 1

www.tigertalesbooks.com

One Christmas Mystery

by

M. Christina Butler

Illustrated by

Tina Macnaughton

tiger tales

It was almost Christmas, and Little Hedgehog was just about ready for his Christmas party.

"I just need my friends to bring the decorations," he beamed.

But when they arrived, Rabbit was very upset.
"There's not a holly berry in sight!" he moaned.
"Even in Holly Grove?" asked Little Hedgehog.
"Come on! We'll look together."

"How strange," puzzled Little Hedgehog when they arrived. "The bushes were full of berries yesterday."

"We'll put these in the bag anyway," said Badger, picking the berries. "Along with this ivy."

"Oh, no!" exclaimed Rabbit. "I forgot the bag!"
"Oh, Rabbit!" sighed Fox.

"Don't worry!" said Little Hedgehog. "We can use my hat."

"Now let's look for pine cones!" said Fox. "There'll be plenty in Evergreen Woods."

But as they walked through the woods, they couldn't see any pine cones.

"Maybe there are some in the higher branches," suggested Little Hedgehog.

So Fox climbed on Badger's shoulders, and Little Hedgehog climbed on top of Fox.

"I found some!" called Little Hedgehog.

Rabbit caught the pine
cones in Little Hedgehog's hat.
"Is that all?" he cried.
But Little Hedgehog gasped.
"I can see Mole from up here,
and he looks upset!"

The friends raced over to Mole.

"What's wrong?" asked Badger.

"It's my scarf," sniffed Mole. "It's missing."

"The one Grandpa Mole made you?" said Rabbit.

Mole nodded. "I hung it out to dry, and now it's gone."

"There's only one thing to do," smiled
Little Hedgehog, emptying his hat and
giving it to Mole to keep him warm.
"We'll help you find your scarf!"

"Where could the scarf be?" wondered
Rabbit. "What happened to it?"
"Maybe someone took it," suggested Fox.
"Took my *special* scarf?" cried Mole.
"We must get it back!"
But as Mole ran off, Little
Hedgehog's hat slid down over
his eyes! He tripped and fell
with a thud.

Everyone rushed over to help.
"I fell into a hole!" cried Mole.
"That's not a hole," declared Fox.
"That's a footprint!"
"Here's another!" called Rabbit.
"And there are squished berries in it!"

"Maybe whoever has all of the holly berries—" started Fox.

"Has my scarf!" finished Mole.

Rabbit inspected the footprint. "Whoever it is certainly has LARGE feet!"

"A big SCARY someone has my scarf," sniffed Mole. "I'll never get it back."

"We'll find it together," comforted Little Hedgehog. "That's what friends are for!"

The friends followed the footprints deeper into the woods.

"I've never been THIS far into the woods before!" said Little Hedgehog.

Suddenly, they came to a huge, dark cave.
Outside the cave on a BIG table was a BIG
mug and a BIG bowl.

"Who lives here?" trembled Mole,
stumbling forward.

As the friends crept closer, they
heard a stomping sound, and the
ground began to shake.
"Those are very loud footsteps!"
exclaimed Badger. "I think we'd better . . ."

"... RUN!"

"Eek!" cried Mole as Little Hedgehog's hat slid down over his eyes again. He stumbled and fell in front of the cave.

"NOOOO!" cried Little Hedgehog.

Out of the cave stomped a BIG, BROWN . . .

. . . BEAR!

Then a baby bear tumbled out after her.

Everyone shivered and shook. Mole pushed the hat out of his eyes.

"Hey!" he squeaked, pointing at the scarf around Baby Bear's neck. "That's mine!"

"It's yours?" asked Mommy Bear. "Baby Bear found it in the woods."

"I'm sorry," sniffled Baby Bear. "We were picking holly berries, and I was cold. I didn't think it belonged to anyone! Here you go."

"We woke up early," added Baby Bear. "And since it's my first Christmas, we decided to have a party. We have plenty of decorations, but not much else."

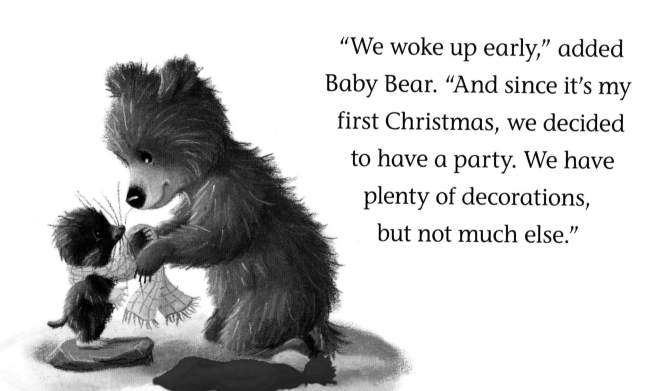

"A party MUST have friends!" cried Little Hedgehog. "Come to my house. We'll celebrate your first Christmas together."

They stuffed as many decorations as they could into Little Hedgehog's hat and headed for home.

At the party, Little Hedgehog had a surprise for Baby Bear. "This is for you," he smiled, giving Baby Bear his stretched-out hat. "It's too big for me now!"

"Looks like we'll be knitting you a new one," chuckled Badger as they all raised their mugs of hot chocolate.

"Hooray to giving, and sharing, and making new friends!" beamed Little Hedgehog. "Merry Christmas!"